DREAM

By Ramón Pressley

Chapter 1

I Would Like You to Meet

The air had the smell and feel of spring warmth on her body as the calm breeze brushed across the lush green grass. "I'm . . . so . . . bored!" Ciara exhaled with a heavy sigh. She was alone on the swing set at the playground in the apartment complex where she lived. The complex was a gated community and she lived on the third floor. The playground was fairly big. It had a yellow tube slide, a wooden ramp leading to a platform that connected to monkey bars,

and two play horses on springs.

Ciara was a nine-year old Hispanic girl with long black hair that she kept in a ponytail, and hazel eyes that sparkled like glass marbles when the light touched them just right. Grown-ups often called her "Cici." She cringed every time she heard the nickname and didn't allow her friends to call her that, except for one friend, Mikey, whom she held dear to her.

Mikey had heard Ciara's mother call her for dinner one day. *"Cici, come home now, mi amor. Supper is ready."* Ciara looked at Mikey, embarrassed by the nickname. She scowled at him, and said, "Don't you ever call me Cici or I'll..."

Before she could finish, he interrupted, "I like it." Ciara was quickly put at ease, as he continued, "Don't worry… it'll be our secret and it will be safe with me." A gigantic smile extended across Ciara's face, and from then on, Mikey was locked away in her heart.

Mikey was a seven-year-old Caucasian boy. The youngest amongst her friends, she noticed several things about him. Everything on his head seemed oversized. He had big, blue eyes that were covered with huge, brown, circle glasses. The lenses made his eyes appear bigger than they really were. He had big teeth with a chipped tooth on the right side of his mouth; plus, he was in desperate need of a visit to the dentist. He had freckles on both sides of his cheeks and an oversized red cap that he wore backwards, because it made him feel like he could move faster.

Mikey had not had use of his legs since birth so he was in a wheelchair. He pushed himself with his strong arms, refusing to be pushed by anyone. Mikey did not consider himself handicapped. He was very bold, confident, and seemed rude at times because he was outspoken. Ciara liked that about him. Eventually, she hardly noticed he was in a wheelchair.

"Hey Ciara!" It was Ramon calling her name as he approached the playground. "Hey Ramon!" She responded as her boredom immediately vanished with the sight of a familiar face.

Ramon was an Afro-American boy. Ciara and her mom couldn't understand how he got the name Ramon, since he wasn't Hispanic and he didn't speak Spanish but after a while his name just seemed to fit him. He was eight-years old and looked as if he belonged on television because of his good looks. His hair was jet black, bloomed out like a cupcake, and was soft to the touch.

He was very smart and had a wonderful imagination, which made playing at the playground the best whenever he was around. He wouldn't speak much if he didn't know you, but couldn't keep quiet if he did. Athletic and quick on his feet, he could out-run any kid who challenged him. Yet he couldn't seem to keep his shoelaces tied. Teachers at school would always make him step out of line just to tie his shoes. Ramon sat on the swing next to Ciara and they began to swing. Then they heard a voice yell out, "Hey ya dumb dummies!"

"Mikeyyy!" Ciara and Ramon yelled out together. They dragged their feet against the sand with every attempt to slow down, jumped off the swings, and ran toward Mikey.

"Chilll! I'm not a superstar! Gosh." Mikey stated. He didn't like too much attention.

"What's up, Mikey?" Ramon asked, as he was the first to approach.

"Hey! What's up, Ramon?"

They high-fived each other as their hands clapped together, then they turned their hands into a handshake. It was obvious that this was their signature greeting.

"Hi Mikey." Ciara said as she trailed behind Ramon, high-fiving Mikey as well. "What took you so long to get here?"

"I would have been here sooner, but my mom made me change out of my school clothes. I swear that woman was a general at one point in her life!" Mikey said jokingly. "Don't swear,

Mikey!" Ciara said sternly. Ciara had a way of chilling Mikey out when he got slick with his words.

The three of them continued talking and enjoying each other's company. Suddenly, from a far-off distance they heard the sweetest sound a child's ear could hear. Their eyes widened as the beautiful melody registered in their minds and filtered the information to their mouths, and they yelled in chorus, "ICE CREAM!!"

Chapter 2

"Yeah, Right"

Ciara, Ramon, and Mikey reacted as any child would. They rushed off toward the sound of the ice cream truck. Ciara and Ramon sought out the truck and arrived together. Without looking back, they knew Mikey would be rolling up behind them. Larry the Ice Cream Man knew the three of them by name and would give them free samples of ice cream at the end of his work day.

"Hello Ramon! Hey Cici! What's up Mikey?!" Larry greeted them as they approached the ice cream truck. "Who's Cici?" Ramon questioned. Ciara and Mikey instantly looked at each other as if they were agreeing to allow Ramon in on their secret. "That's my nickname," Ciara said agitatedly. "That's for babies! And you better not tell anybody or call me by that name! GOT IT?"

Uncertain about answering, he replied, "Oookay! Calm down, Sista!"

Larry chuckled and quickly directed their attention to another topic.

"I wish I could give you kids a free sample of ice cream, but I'm sold out today." The three of them looked at Larry as if he were joking, but the look on his face told them it was true. Their faces quickly went from delight to disappointment. *"But, I do have something for you guys."* Larry backed away from the side window and disappeared to the back of the truck. They could do nothing but wait in suspense. Larry returned with an orange balloon floating in the air with a string attached. *"I have one balloon, but…"*

"How you gonna come here with no ice cream and only one balloon?" Mikey interrupted. Ramon stayed quiet but had a look of agreement with him. Ciara gave a sharp look to Mikey and said his name as if she were a big sister.

"Mikey!"

"I'm just sayin!"

Larry chuckled again. *"It's okay, Cici, Mikey is right, but this isn't your ordinary balloon. This balloon is magical. Once I give you kids this balloon, you can be anything you want to be, do anything you want to do, and go anywhere your heart desires! But the magic only works when you share the balloon."*

"Yeah, right!" Ramon blurted, not persuaded.

Ciara and Ramon were looking at Larry as if he had lost his mind. Mikey, on the other hand, was intrigued. His big, blue eyes widened and his ears grasped onto every word Larry was saying. He leaned forward, his mouth opened slightly, and he softly said, "Whoa . . ." Larry reached out to the side of the truck to hand them the balloon. Mikey was the only one to reach out. Just then Larry pulled the balloon back towards him.

"Would you like to know the balloon's name?"

"The balloon has a name?" Ramon asked.

"Of course!"

"Well, what is the balloon's name?"

"I would like you to meet Dream," he said as he placed Dream into Mikey's hand. *"I have to run. I'll talk with you kids later. Have fun and protect Dream."*

Chapter 3

Prepare for Takeoff

With Dream in his hand, Mickey could not seem to take his eyes off Dream's bright orange color. "Come on. Let's go back to the playground." Ciara said. Without saying a word, Ramon accompanied her. The two of them walked towards the playground, but Mikey did not follow. He looked up at Dream and said, "Dream, if it's okay with you, I'm going to place you right here on my handle. Don't worry, I won't go too fast." He turned sideways, faced his handle, and tied Dream. "Okay, hold on!"

He headed towards the playground to catch up with Ciara and Ramon. Once he arrived, he wheeled himself off the sidewalk and onto the grass. He noticed a look of dismay on their faces. "What's wrong with you guys?"

"No ice cream." Ciara answered.

"Yeah, man. No ice cream." Ramon agreed.

"Man, forget about the ice cream. Dream says we have to go!"

"Go? Who said that?" Ciara asked perplexed.

"Dream. You can't hear her?"

"Dream is a girl?"

"Uh . . . yeah!"

"Hey, I can hear her, too!" Ramon voiced excitedly. "She says we have to get to the star ship!"

Mikey leaned forward in his wheelchair in awe and said, "The . . . star ship?"

"Yeah! Come on, you guys!" Ramon said, jumping to his feet. Mikey looked up at Dream, smiled, and followed Ramon. Ciara didn't know what to say, so she decided not to say anything. She stood up and followed the boys.

Ramon ran to the swing set and announced, "Welcome to the Comet Star Ship! Please have a seat and prepare for takeoff!" Mikey gazed with amazement at the swings, which was now the "Comet Star Ship."

"Commander Ramon, Lieutenant Mikey, Sergeant Dream, let's prepare for takeoff!" Ciara chimed in.

Mikey could not contain his thrill. "Roger, Air Chief!"

He rolled his wheelchair to the middle swing that Ramon was holding for him. He lifted himself from his chair onto the swing. He untied Dream and then tied her to the swing's chain link. Ramon ensured that Mikey was seated and sat in the swing next to him. Ciara pushed the wheelchair out of the way and sat on the other side of Mikey.

"Comet Star Ship pilots are you ready for takeoff?"

"Ready, Air Chief!" Ramon and Mikey responded at the same time.

"Is Sergeant Dream locked in?"

Mikey tugged on the string, reassuring she was secured. "Locked in and ready, Air Chief!"

"Commander Ramon, we're ready for takeoff!"

"Roger! All systems go!"

"Shhh …Tick." Ciara made a machine sound moving her hand to Mikey's swing.

"Shhh …Tick." Ramon made a similar sound following Ciara's lead.

Mikey didn't notice that Ciara and Ramon were holding onto his swing. He didn't want to take his eyes away from the ravishing clear, blue sky.

"COMET START SHIP WILL LAUNCH IN . . .TEN . . . NINE . . . EIGHT . . . SEVEN. . ." Ramon shouted and started shaking Mikey's swing. "Rumble, Rumble, Rumble…" Ciara made jet blaster sounds while shaking the other side of Mikey's swing.

"SIX . . . FIVE . . . FOUR . . ." Ramon counted down.

The three of them leaned back in their swings, holding on tightly to the chains. Ciara and Ramon stretched out their legs in front of them. They leaned forward as the swings drifted backwards, leaning backwards as the swings drifted forward. They repeated this motion as the swings began to gain momentum. "THREE . . . TWO . . . ONE . . . WE HAVE LIFT OFF!"

Ramon roared.

Ciara and Ramon pumped their legs back and forth, still holding on to Mikey's swing. They swung higher, higher, and higher. Once they soared above the ground, they let the swings glide. They looked at Dream, admiring the sunlight beaming through her radiant orange color as she glided with them. The three friends drifted through the air as Dream took them on a dazzling voyage to the moon.

Chapter 4

The Race

That night, Ciara and Ramon agreed that Mikey should take Dream home. They felt it was the best place for her to be. The following day, the three of them couldn't wait to get back to the playground to see where Dream would take them next. Ramon gulped down the breakfast his father prepared, slipped on his sneakers without tying them, and kissed his mother on the cheek. "*Tie your shoes, baby.*" Ramon's mother warned. He ran out the door as it closed behind him.

Jogging towards the playground, he saw Mikey and Dream heading to the playground as well. As Mikey saw, Ramon running, he began to roll faster. When Ramon noticed, Mikey moving faster than him, he went from a jog to a full sprint. A race to the playground was on!

"Hold on, Dream!" Mikey said as he moved his arms faster, rolling at his top speed. Mikey and Ramon arrived at the playground nearly at the same time. It was now a debate as to who arrived first. Ciara was already there. She noticed the commotion between the boys as she walked over to them.

"Ciara, who got here first, me or Ramon?" Mikey demanded.

"I don't know. I didn't see the race," she replied.

"You just don't wanna hurt Ramon's feelings. Okay then, who's faster, Ramon or me?"

"I really didn't see who got here first. And who's faster between you and Ramon? I don't know that either."

"I'm the champion!" Ramon blurted, pumping his fist in the air.

"Ha! Champion, my booty butt! I whooped you and you know it!" They went back and forth debating until Ciara came up with an idea.

"Why don't you guys race again?"

Accepting the challenge, Ramon responded, "That's a great idea! Let's do it!"

Casually Mikey replied, "Alright . . . but I don't see the point. You're gonna lose anyway!" They headed to the end of the street across from the playground and Ciara went over the rules.

"Okay. You guys are gonna race from here to the end of the road and back. First one to the finish line wins!"

Ramon and Mikey agreed as if they were racing for the world championship. "Mikey untie Dream and give her to me. She'll be our start and finish flag." Ciara said. Once Mikey handed Dream over to Ciara, she noticed something different about her. Purple eyes with long eyelashes and a warming smile.

"Dream! She has a face!"

"Do you like it? I had my mom put it on her so we can see what she looks like."

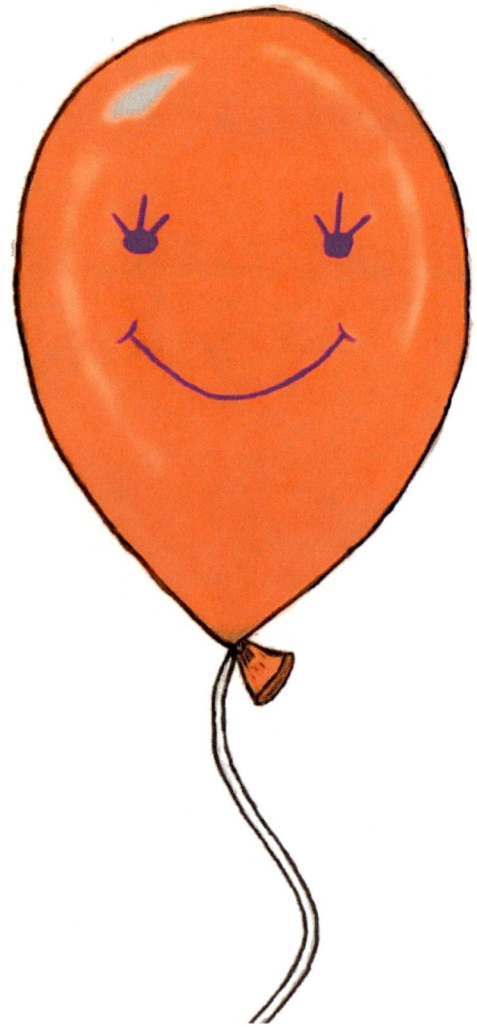

"I love it! She's beautiful."

Mikey turned his attention back to Ramon. "I'm sorry to be the one to tell you this brotha, but you're goin down!"

"We shall see about that, my friend!"

"ON YOUR MARK!" Ciara shouted.

They gazed down the road, not allowing their concentration to be broken.

Feeling uneasy, Ciara said, "Um . . . Ramon, you may wanna tie your shoes."

Focused on the race, he didn't seem to hear her request. She didn't bother to ask again. He was always running with them untied anyway.

"GET SET!"

Ramon leaned forward with his legs and arms bent. His hands formed into a fist, but he was relaxed and ready for takeoff. Mikey gripped the wheels to his chair, leaning forward anticipating Ciara's final command.

"GO!" Ciara shouted, waving Dream up and down. They took off. Mikey pulled in front of Ramon fast, but Ramon wasn't too far behind. He ran up next to Mikey, quickly realizing he was nowhere near his full speed. He glanced at Mikey, observed his arms pumping and rolling his wheels at his max speed. He had a look of determination to win. Ramon slowed his pace slightly enough to get behind Mikey.

"Ha! Eat my dust!" Mikey teased, excited to be ahead. Suddenly, he felt a slight nudge on the back of his wheelchair. His arms couldn't keep up with the rotation of the wheels. He didn't bother to look back; he knew Ramon had taken hold of his handles, pushing him at an unbelievable speed. Mikey closed his eyes, tilted his head back, raised his arms above his head, and delightfully cheered, "Yeahhh!!"

Ramon smiled and shouted, "Mikey, what are you doin' bro? You have to steer your racecar!" Mikey quickly opened his eyes, pushing his oversized cap over his eyebrows as if it were the visor on a racecar helmet. He stuck out his arms in front of him and balled his fist as if he were gripping a steering wheel. His wheelchair was transformed into a racecar and Ramon his

Pit Crew Leader.

"Mikey, there's a hard left up ahead. Get ready." Ramon warned.

"Copy."

"Readyyy . . . Left!"

Mikey leaned his torso to the right, turning his fists with the right over the left, his lips tightened, and his head cocked to the left. "SKURRTTT!!!" Ramon made the screeching sound of burning rubber. "Woohoo!" Mikey cheered overjoyed, straightening out his arms after the turn. They circled a section of the apartment complex and headed back towards Ciara and Dream. Ramon, short of breath from the endless running, said,

"Mikey . . . one . . . last . . . turn to your right, and you're home free!"

"Roger."

"Now, Mikey! Turn right! SKURRTTT!"

Mikey turned his fists with the left over the right, his torso bent to the left, his head cocked to the right. "The finish line! I see it!" Mikey shouted.

"All right! Step on it! The other racecars are coming up on you fast!"

Mikey tucked his chin, shrugged his shoulders, and extended his arms a little further to show that he was ready for more speed. Ramon observed Mikey's actions and gave it everything he had to go faster. Ciara noticed what they were up to and began to wave Dream up and down as if she was the finish line checkered flag.

"Vrooommm!!" Ramon made the sound of the racecar passing the finish line. Ciara began to jump up and down with excitement like a cheerleader, clapping while holding onto Dream's string.

"THAT WAS TOTALLY AWESOME!" Mikey shouted.

Ramon gradually stopped Mikey. They gave each other a high five. He walked towards the playground exhausted and lay on the grass, seeking to catch his breath. Ciara and Mikey headed towards Ramon. Ciara sat next to him. She looked up at Mikey and noticed that he had a look of fulfillment on his face. She grinned and handed Dream to Mikey. He tied Dream back onto his wheelchair then slid himself out and onto the ground. The three of them lay back on the grass with their hands behind their heads, gazing at the infinite blue above.

The breeze moved the sky's cotton to look like different characters the human mind could only imagine.

Chapter 5

What Do You Want to Be

After a moment of silence, Mikey asked, "What do you guys want to be when you grow up?" Ciara didn't have to think about it. "I want to be a teacher, because I want my own desk with an apple on it and I want to teach children different things so they can do better things in the world."

Ramon felt it was his turn to answer, "I want to be a dentist. I wanna take care of people's teeth. Mikey, you can be my first patient."

Mikey placed his tongue on his chipped tooth and asked, "What's wrong with my teeth?" Ciara and Ramon chuckled in response to Mikey's question.

"What do you want to be, Mikey?" Ramon asked.

"I want to be a racecar driver . . . The fastest one that ever lived!"

~Silence~

"Coool!" the three of them said admiring one an other's answers.

As they continued lying on the grass, Dream danced with the wind and then, without warning, SNAP! The wind caused Dream's string to break apart. "OH NO!" the three of them yelled. In an instant, Ramon sprung to his feet and ran towards Dream in an effort to rescue her. He leaped for the small portion of her strand that was still attached, but was unable to curl his fingers around the thin twine as it slipped off his fingertips.

The breeze carried Dream further and further away. Ciara swiftly helped Mikey into his wheelchair, and ran to catch up with Ramon. The puff of air carried Dream up and over the rooftop of the apartment complex. They were losing sight of her. Ramon yelled franticly,

"CIARA, RUN UP THE STAIRS AND TELL ME IF YOU SEE DREAM!"

She ran up to the third floor. Out of breath, her eyes moved from side to side, scanning the area with every effort to locate her. She felt a tingle in the pit of her stomach and she could feel the beat of her heart. Suddenly, her eyes widened when she spotted Dream's bright orange color and yelled, "THERE SHE IS!"

"WHERE, CICI, WHERE?!" Ramon shouted.

She pointed to the gate. She realized that she liked the nickname Cici in a time like this. She quickly shook it off as she came to her senses and bellowed, "HER STRING IS CAUGHT ON THE GATE AT THE CORNER OF THE COMPLEX! HURRY RAMON!"

Ramon bolted towards the main gate as Ciara scampered down the stairs. As he got closer to the gate, he stopped in the middle of the road. He looked right and saw Mikey rolling his wheelchair in his direction.

"THERE SHE IS, RAMON!" Mikey wailed.

Ramon looked left and saw Dream swaying in the air, her string still caught on the gate. Without hesitation, he jetted towards her. Stretching his legs to the max, he could feel every stride his legs were making. His arms were moving like wheels on a locomotive. He barely felt his feet touching the earth. As he got closer to Dream, however, something unusual happened to him. He felt a jolt throughout his body. His right leg was trying to move forward, but it felt stuck. His arms were no longer wheels on a locomotive. Rather, they thrust in front of him, bracing for impact. He gasped as he fell to the ground. He had stumbled over his untied shoelaces! Tumbling forward to the pavement, he curled into a ball and rolled onto his back. Then, surprised, he was able to pop back up to his feet. He attempted to regain his speed, but realized that wasn't needed. He was already close enough to the gate where Dream was caught. A strong gust blew and untangled her. He leaped onto the gate using one foot to propel him up in another attempt to grasp her. Reaching out, fully extending his arm, his fingers closed like a vice grip in hopes of

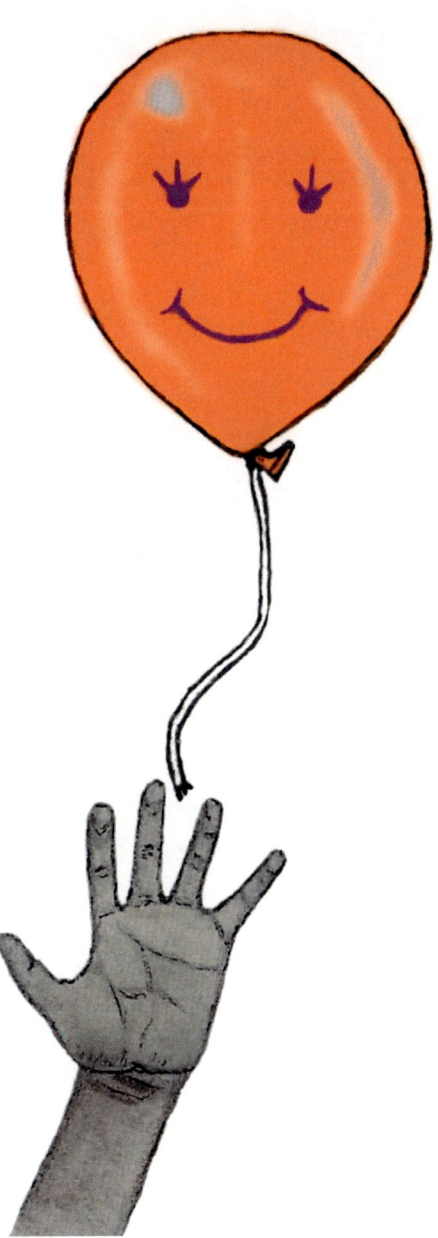

grabbing her strand.

    Dream smiled at the three of them as her face turned slowly away. She allowed the breeze to take her up, up, and up. Ciara, Ramon, and Mikey yelled at the same time, "Nooo!!!"

    There was nothing further Ramon could do but keep his eyes on Dream. He climbed down from the gate. Ciara walked up beside him with tears flooding her eyes. Mikey slowly rolled up beside them. "No! Come back, Dream!" Mikey begged. The three of them watched their best friend soar away. They did not take their teary eyes off Dream until she was out of sight. Without speaking a word, they headed back to the playground, ever so often looking up, hoping Dream would return. Once they arrived they plopped down on the grass.

"Are you okay?" Ciara asked Ramon, concerned about his fall.

"I'm fine."

Without being instructed, he pulled his legs to his chest, and tied his shoes. The three sat in silence, still looking up for Dream.

Chapter 6

Flight of Fancy

"Vroom . . . Vrooom . . . Vrooommm!" Mikey was making a racecar sound. His arms extended in front of him and his hands were pretending to grip a steering wheel. Ciara and Ramon looked at Mikey, who seemed as if he didn't care that Dream was gone.

"What are you doin', bro? Dream is gone!" Ramon said puzzled.

"No, she's not, I can still hear her and she says we gotta go!" Mikey said lightheartedly.

"Hey, I hear her too!" Ciara shouted. Feeling encouraged, she ran towards the swing set. "Comet Star Ship pilots, let's prepare for takeoff!" Slowly, Ramon stood up and wiped his tears onto his shirt sleeve. A smile grew on Ramon's and Mikey's faces as they responded, "Roger, Air Chief!"

Ramon grabbed the handles of Mikey's wheelchair and pushed him to the swing set. The three of them got onto their swings.

"Ready for takeoff, Air Chief!" Ramon and Mikey shouted. The three of them counted down, "TEN . . . NINE . . . EIGHT . . . SEVEN . . . SIX . . . FIVE . . . FOUR . . . THREE . . . TWO . . . ONE . . .

MISSION CATCHING DREAM, WE HAVE LIFT OFF!"

Dream's magic not only created their dreams, but guided those dreams to the stars and beyond.

"Dreams fade but are never gone…just check <u>your</u> lost and found."

~Ramón Pressley

The state of being united or joined.

UNITY

Made in the USA
Middletown, DE
02 June 2017